Russia

ASIA

China

Istanbul

Japan

Thailand

AFRICA

Kenya

AUSTRALIA

My Granny Went to Market
A Round-the-World Counting Rhyme

written by Stella Blackstone

illustrated by Christopher Corr

Barefoot Books
Celebrating Art and Story

My granny went to market
to buy a flying carpet.

She bought the flying carpet
from a man in Istanbul.
It was trimmed with yellow tassels,
and made of knotted wool.

Next she went to Thailand
and flew down from the sky
to buy herself two temple cats,
Puyin and Puchai. *

*'Puyin' means little girl 'Puchai' means little boy

Then she headed westwards
to the land of Mexico;
she bought three fierce and funny masks,
one pink, one blue, one yellow.

The flying carpet seemed to know
exactly where to take her;
they went to China next,
to buy four lanterns made of paper.*

*the symbol on the lanterns means 'double happiness'

'To Switzerland!' cried Granny
as the carpet turned around.
She bought five cowbells there,
that made a funny clanking sound.

'Now Africa!' sang Granny,
'We must wake the morning sun!'
They spiralled south to Kenya
where she bought six booming drums.

Next they travelled northwards,
past the homes of mountain trolls,
to stop a while in Russia
for seven nesting dolls.

'Australia,' Granny ordered,
'Take me down to Alice Springs.
I want eight buzzing boomerangs
that fly back without wings.'

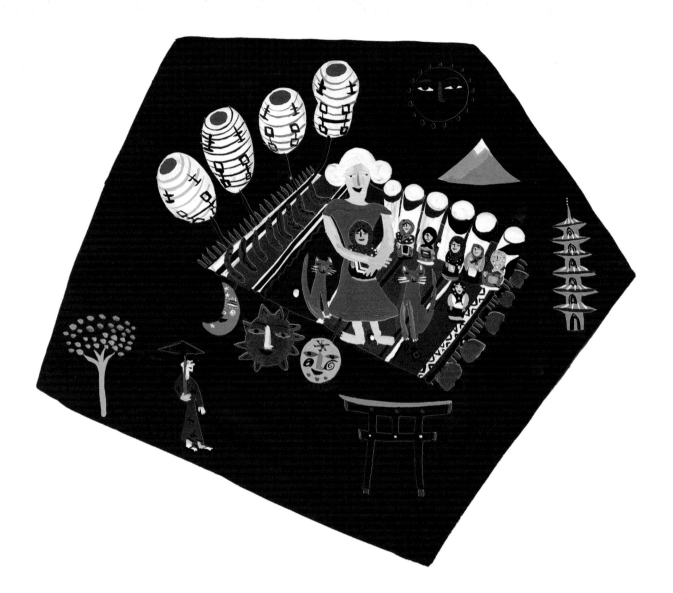

Then Granny sighed, 'I've bought so much,
but nothing Japanese!'
In Tokyo she found nine kites
that fluttered in the breeze.

But best of all, she met me
in the mountains of Peru,
where she gave me ten black llamas
and a magic carpet too!

And I flew away to . . . .

one carpet 1

two cats 2

three masks 3

four lanterns 4

five cowbells 5

six drums 6

seven nesting dolls 7

eight boomerangs 8

nine kites 9

ten llamas 10

For Felix — S. B.
For Eva Sugrue, my grandmother — C. C.

Barefoot Books
124 Walcot Street
Bath BA1 5BG

First published in Great Britain in 2005 by Barefoot Books Ltd

This book was typeset in Kosmik
The illustrations were prepared in gouache on Fabriano paper

Graphic design by Louise Millar
Colour separation by Grafiscan, Verona
Printed and bound in Hong Kong by South China Printing Co. Ltd

This book has been printed on 100% acid-free paper

Hardback ISBN 1-84148-791-0

British Cataloguing-in-Publication Data:
a catalogue record for this book is available from the British Library

1 3 5 7 9 8 6 4 2

Barefoot Books
Celebrating Art and Story

At Barefoot Books, we celebrate art and story with books that open
the hearts and minds of children from all walks of life, inspiring them to read
deeper, search further, and explore their own creative gifts. Taking our
inspiration from many different cultures, we focus on themes that encourage
independence of spirit, enthusiasm for learning, and acceptance of other
traditions. Thoughtfully prepared by writers, artists and storytellers from
all over the world, our products combine the best of the present with the best
of the past to educate our children as the caretakers of tomorrow.

www.barefootbooks.com

EUROPE

Switzerland

NORTH AMERICA

Mexico

SOUTH
Peru AMERICA

Istanbul to Thailand
Thailand to Mexico
Mexico to China
China to Switzerland
Switzerland to Kenya
Kenya to Russia
Russia to Australia
Australia to Japan
Japan to Peru